What is steampunk?

The simplest definition is Victorian era science fiction. H.G. Wells, Jules Verne, Edgar Allan Poe, and Mark Twain, among others, were the forerunners of the genre.

What is tea dueling?

Tea dueling is a parlor game of cunning and concentration in which two combatants square off armed only with tea and biscuits. It requires a quick wit and a steady hand.
The rules are simple, but the techniques and strategies are as varied and unique as the combatants themselves.

Alternative and additional rules will have you rolling on the floor, literally.

From the after hours Chicago salons to the dirt streets of Old Tucson at high noon. From the sun kissed, gently swaying deck of the Queen Mary ocean liner to the most fashionable of New York City's skyline addresses. From the bombastic burlesque brigades of Atlanta's finest to the darkest denizens, mechanical monstrosities, and industrial revolutionaries of a past that never was. From the convention halls to your parlor. Tea dueling can take place anywhere.

You will learn the fine art of the duel from world renowned champions of this steampunk pastime. Khurt Khave, aka the Dirty Weasel, despite his motto of, "Cheat to win!" will disclose his tried and true secrets, all within the bounds of the rules, if not propriety, that will insure you are victorious every time.

Here follow the rules as laid down in the more civilized, American-speaking parts of the world. We shall cut through the cacophonic buffoonery and you will see tea dueling as played by the professionals.

We refer to the tea dueling weapons as biscuits. This is merely a formality of tradition which has been retained from the old timey days. We, the global cultural leaders, refer to them by their proper name, cookies. But for the sake of nostalgia and presumptuousness, we shall refer to them within this context as biscuits. And if you spell it "bisquit" you are just an outright contemptible ignoramus.

Quick start guide:
1. Tea
2. Biscuits
3. Dunk
4. *Last* one to eat their biscuit wins!

You may add whatever pomp and circumstance you deem fit. Make up completely arbitrary and unnecessary titles for yourselves. Award prizes. Everyone loves prizes.

1. PREPARE THE TEA. We will assume the Host of the dueling event is knowledgeable in the means and methods of steeping tea. That will not be covered here. If you cannot yet brew tea then you are not ready to duel! If using a newfangled steampunk contraption which measures the temperature, it should remain at 190 degrees Fahrenheit or greater.
The tea must be kept hot to insure the proper combat-ready conditions of the biscuit.

2. SET OUT BISCUITS. A serving tray is best. A nice platter will do. A paper plate is right out! Have some class. The preferred biscuit is the Pepperidge Farm chessmen. Lay out four to eight biscuits, depending on the size of the serving piece. Gluten-free and sugar-free variants are not suitable for dueling as their molecular structure is different and the cookie doesn't crumble adequately. Watching tea drip; same idiom as watching paint dry.

3. CHOOSE YOUR WEAPON. Each combatant shall choose a biscuit. Etiquette states that a lady shall choose first in the case of male-female combatants. In the case of an officially issued challenge, propriety of first choice of weapon shall go to the challengee, the combatant who was challenged. Otherwise the Host shall decide who chooses first.

CowGirtler Photography

4. DUNK! When the Host says, "Ready!" the combatants will hold their biscuit above their tea, using only their thumb and index finger. At the decree of, "Dunk!" the adversaries shall lower their biscuits into their tea. At least half of the biscuit must be submerged. If an opponent fails to dunk in a timely manner, or does not sink their biscuit to the proper depth, a violation is called. New weapons are chosen and the duel begins again. A second infraction of dousing indiscretion results in the forfeit of the offending combatant.

When it has been determined that both combatants have made a viable dunk, the Host shall make an audible, robust count to five. After which the competitors shall remove their biscuit from the tea.

5. VICTORY. The *LAST* combatant to cleanly eat the entire biscuit is declared the winner. Minor external crumbage and/or biscuit loss is allowable as determined by the Host. With a Damage Ratio no greater than 7% being acceptable.

If part or all of the biscuit falls into the tea, it is a splash. The splasher is beaten.

If part or all of the biscuit falls onto the table or surrounding area, it is a splatter. The splatterer is beaten.

If part or all of the biscuit falls onto the dunker, it is a splodge. The splodger is beaten and shamed.

If neither combatant is successful in eating their biscuit, then another weapon is chosen and the duel begins again!

VARIANT RULES

Cutthroat or 3-Way - Three combatants, each with a single biscuit. Standard rules of engagement.

Double Dunk - Standard - each combatant duels with a biscuit in each hand. The biscuits are dunked at the same time. A single cup can be used for both biscuits if it will accommodate both biscuits. Or two cups can be used, one for each biscuit.

Double Dunk - Dominator - each combatant duels with two biscuits in one hand. The biscuits cannot touch. Traditional holding style is one biscuit held between the thumb and ring finger and the other biscuit held between the index and middle finger.

2-on-1 - Single Biscuit - two combatants versus a single combatant, each with a single biscuit. The solitary combatant must defeat both opponents to be victorious.

2-on-1 - Double Biscuit - two combatants, each with a single biscuit, versus a single combatant who has two biscuits. The solitary combatant can use either the standard or dominator methods of double dunking, and must defeat both opponents to be victorious.

Last Man Nomming - A free-for-all of four or more duelists, each with a single biscuit. Every combatant for themselves. Standard rules of engagement.

CowGirlZen Photography

Steamroller - Each combatant lies on their stomach opposing each other, face to face. Their tea cups are placed in front of them. After dunking, the opponents must each do a full roll. At the Host's discretion, additional rolls must be made on command.

Masquerade - Each combatant must wear a mask which covers their entire face. This increases the difficulty of a clean nom.

King of the Hill - You must have a hill. Though a staircase or steep ramp can be substituted. The opponents start at the bottom of the hill, dunk, then run to the top of the hill. The victor is the one who eats their biscuit last atop the hill.

Crossdunking – Each combatant dunks their biscuit in their opponent's cup.

Biscuit Dancing - Can be used for taunting purposes or the combatants may be called upon to dance by the Host should the cookies not crumble in a timely manner. Also called fig jigging or cookie shakin'.

Biscuit Dancing - Hokey Pokey variant - You put your biscuit hand in, you put your biscuit hand out, you put your biscuit hand in and you shake it all about.

Best Out Of 3 - Usually reserved for grudge matches, this allows the drama, and insults, to be drawn out for the delight of all!

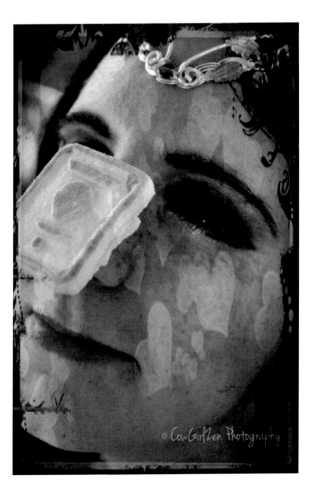

Biscuit Balancing - Each combatant must balance a biscuit on their nose. Whichever opponent drops their biscuit first must dunk for a count of 8 instead of 5. For the more advanced duelists, a standard dunk can be performed before the balancing. The cookie cannot be touched after it has been placed upon the nose. The combatant must either flip, slide, shake, or otherwise cajole the biscuit into their mouth. Use of the tongue is allowed in this variant. Standard duel victory conditions apply.

Blind Fury - Each combatant is blindfolded. They must use their in-tea-ition to decide when the best time is to consume the biscuit. Can be played in two-person teams in which the second person is not blindfolded and tells the dunker when to eat the biscuit.

Aces High - A deck of cards is required. Each combatant draws a card from the top of the deck. The one who draws the lowest card must stand up, spin around twice, then return to their seat. If it is a tie, each one draws a new card. The competition continues in this manner until there is a winner.

"We're all mad here. I'm mad. You're mad."

Musical Chairs - Two chairs are present. Each opponent must stand, dunk, then move around the table until the music stops, then take the nearest chair. Should the biscuits remain steadfast, the music may be started again at the Host's whim. The biscuit can only be eaten when seated and no music is playing. More than two can participate but this becomes very splodgey.

Topsy Turvy - Each combatant lies on their back, head to head but adjusted so that they can see their opponent. Their tea cup is placed on the ground just above their head. Dunking and victory conditions remain the same.
WARNING: Don't drip tea in your eye, that's one of the reasons you should have goggles. Steampunk is dangerous!

Globetrotter Gambit - Each duelist must stand, turn away from their tea cup, then dunk behind their back. Standard rules and playing style then apply.

Irish Rules Variant - full contact tea dueling. Not for those with delicate sensibilities.

© CowGirlJen Photography

Tag Team - Two teams consisting of two duelists face off. The Host determines the format:

1. 1-on-1 - Single combatant from each team. Standard duel.

2. 2-on-2 - Both combatants from each team. Each dunks. In the event that each team scores a clean nom, the victor from each team engages in a second duel.

3. Tag Team - Single combatant from each team. Best out of 3 (or 5, or 7!) with each team member rotating or "tagging out" for each duel.

4. Elimination - Can be played with teams of two, three, or more. Standard duel. The winner stays in. The loser is eliminated. The team that runs out of players first, loses.

"Off with
their heads!"

Tag Team With Cup Hats - Standard Tag Team rules apply,
except that one member from each team must wear a full
tea cup on their head while their fellow team member(s)
duels from above!

WARNING: Do not overfill the tea dueling cup-bonnet.
Perhaps it is best to pour the tea first, then don the dueling
bonnet (or dueling chapeau for you too manly men).

MAD TEA DUELING VARIANTS

"Clean cup! Move down!" Duelists must switch seats in a clockwise rotation.

"All ways here are the Queen's way!" The Queen decides how the tea is prepared and declares any rule variants as well as how and when they are applied.

Ravens and Writing Desks - The duelists must each recite aloud (or read aloud, for the less learned) "The Raven" by Edgar Allan Poe. When done reciting, the first clean nommer wins.

"Off with their heads!" Each combatant must bite off the head of their chessman before dunking, then completely submerge the remainder of their biscuit.

"It's always tea-time, and we've no time to wash the things between whiles."

Mad Tea - Add treacle or butter to your tea. Avoid crumbs.

"You are old, Father William, the young man said." Stand on your head. Duel.

Duchess Delicacy - The Duchess only takes her tea with peppered bacon.

Jabberwocky - Both manxome foes must burble 'til their biscuit gyres and gimbles.

Flamingo Flippancy - The duelists must each stand on one foot, like a flamingo. Wing flapping of the non-biscuit-holding arm is at the Host's discretion.

Caucus Race - The combatants must all run in a sort of circle, beginning and leaving off when they like.

Croquet Challenge - Each combatant must take a croquet mallet and strike a ball, assuming there is a croquet set available and the Queen has invited them to play.

Tarts
CANNOT
be substituted
for biscuits!

Queen of Hearts - A deck of cards is required. After dunking, each combatant draws a card from the top of the deck. The opponent with the lowest card must stand, then bow/curtsy to the Queen if she is present (in which case you must also state boisterously, "Yes, your majesty!"), then to their adversary, then to the host. A duelist who draws the Queen of Hearts automatically wins if they proceed with a clean nom.

Bandersnatchers - With a command of, "1, 2, 3, snatch!" each combatant must quickly grab a biscuit from the tray. The duel then proceeds as normal except that the slower outgraber must dunk for a count of 8, while the faster one only has to dunk to the standard count of 5.

Eat me! - Each duelist must hold three biscuits together, dunk for a count of 10, then duel.

Through The Looking Glass - Each combatant must dunk and duel with their less-dominant hand.

No mock turtles. No mock dunking!

DIRTY WEASEL TIPS & TRICKS

All the bad stuff comes at the end of the book, right? The dark literary basement, seedy back alley brewers, street dueling.

Nobody likes a gloating combatant. But the Dirty Weasel doesn't care. He's a jerk. But he's also a winner. And everybody loves a winner. Here are some of the classic Weasel tips and tricks that can make you a winner, too!

JOIN THE WEASEL POSSE TODAY!

You can't spell CHEAT without TEA

WEASEL TIPS

1. Biscuit selection - a thicker biscuit area does not soggify as quickly. The rook or knight are the best.

2. Tea preparation - cream, sugar, honey, they all serve to cool the tea. There is debate on the effectiveness of this strategy.

3. Stirring - agitation disperses heat.

4. Proper dunking technique - the only time I lost was my first duel for this very reason. Never dunk more than 50% of your biscuit or you will lose!

5. Some like to blow on their biscuit to cool it as well as force off extra dripping soppiness. This is perfectly legal. Its effectiveness is questionable. Just ask Jostling Jocelynne.

6. Some will even shake off extra drops of tea. Don't do this! Unless you're dueling me, then go right ahead. Because only an idiot would perform such a maneuver.

7. Movement is easy as long as you maintain the biscuit in a good vertical position.

8. Play the fool! The more your opponent laughs the more their biscuit shakes.

9. Try to make out with your opponent. This may leave them literally reeling. Or you might get to kiss a hotty (hot-tea)!

10. Tea. Duel. Make friends. Make enemies. Have fun! The crowd will love you. And that's all that really counts.

DIRTY TRICKS

1.Tea flicking - Dipping a finger into your tea and flicking it in your opponent's face. Careful not to burn your finger.

2. Cookie Moshing - Attempting to smash your opponent's cookie with your own.

3. Weaseldunk (Crossdunk Without Permission) - Dunking your biscuit in your opponent's cup.

4. Eat your biscuit early before dunking. It allows your over creamed and sugared tea to cool even faster than that of your opponent. Bad form? I don't care. I love cookies.

5. Call for a corset inspection! They could be hiding *anything* in there. It just so happens that I know the local corset inspector. For a small fee, I can assure that he is at your next tea dueling event.

6. Flirty Khurty - I cannot stress enough the importance of flirting. Whether they are flattered or repulsed, play it to the hilt! There is a surprisingly large number of saloon girls who enjoy the pastime of tea dueling. And they only want an alpha dunker.

7. Chair Mounting - Stand on your chair. Intimidate your opponent. Look down their cleavage. Threaten to drip tea or splodge on them. I personally like to lean back on two legs to demonstrate my superior balance and tea dueling abilities.

8. Put poison or diarrhetic in your opponent's tea. This may be illegal in some places. Perhaps I should have stated a "mild" poison, but I'll leave that up to you.

9. Whatever you do, don't "accidentally" bump the table while your opponent is dunking, thus splashy-saturating their biscuit at a greater ratio than 50%.

10. Showboating is encouraged! The audience will be eating out of your hand, just as long as you're not. My twerking prowess and my trademark Tap Dat Ass maneuver are steampunk world famous.

PRO TECHNIQUES

Statue of Liberty - Pose like the Statue of Liberty.

Big Ben or Tick-Tock - Invert your biscuit and swing it like a clock pendulum.

Rabbit or Hippity-Hop - Move your biscuit up and down like a rabbit.

Jareth's Crystal Ball - Whip your biscuit around like that one scene in Labyrinth. Bonus nothing points for singing while doing it, "You remind me of the babe." Double bonus nothing points if you actually jump during the jump part of the song.

Frere Jacques/Where is Biscuit? - Hide your biscuit while singing the nursery rhyme.

Sign of the Cross - just remember to be the last to nom the Communion biscuit.

Pinky Wave - Literal. Throw in a, "yoohoo!"

Lasso - Wave your biscuit in the air like a lasso. Be sure to yell out, "Yippee Ki Yay!"

Do You Like Scary Movies? - Make hacking, slashing, and chopping motions. Not for amateurs! You can simulate these horror tropes with hand movements while maintaining your biscuit at a stable level.

We Do The Weird Stuff - Yep. Lewd gestures. This [biscuit] is not the hammer.

"Curiouser and curiouser!"

Cool Breeze - Blow on your biscuit to cool it down. Be seductive about it! Or, if you have halitosis, blow across your biscuit towards your opponent. Though this may legally be considered assault, so your opponent might knock you out fo' reals in self defense.

Interpretive Dance of Ancient Folktales - Lots of Mysterious Sunsets ("Where does it go?") and World Floods.

FOOD FOR YOUR TEA PARTY

Any game bird from a local caucus race will do nicely for a main course, though they do tend to be rather dry. Borogove or jubub will suffice, but dodo is highly recommended. Though mutton or jerked jabberwock is a fine substitute for fowl.

Ingredients:
1 dodo bird, full size
1 cup of flutterby crumbs
Lots of rath bacon

At brillig, cook it with fire! Ready the fire pit.
Stuff the dodo with flutterby crumbs and as much rath bacon as you can fit inside.
Run the spit through the dodo and balance it on the rotisserie.
Cook for approximately four hours.
Baste with treacle glaze.

SWEET POTATO SALAD

Ingredients:

4 large sweet potatoes ½ cup mayonnaise
½ Greek yogurt ½ cup diced scallions
1 red or green pepper 2 teaspoons apple cider vinegar
2 teaspoons orange zest salt and pepper to taste
orange segments, optional ½ cup cooked bacon, optional

Directions:
Peel and cube sweet potatoes. Boil in pot until tender.
Drain and set aside to cool off.
In a medium bowl mix all ingredients but potatoes.
Add potatoes to mixture once cooled.
Tastes best chilled.

PASTA SALAD

Ingredients:

2 cups pasta 2 tablespoons dijon mustard
½ cup diced tomatoes ½ cup balsamic vinaigrette dressing
1 can black or green olives ½ cup diced red onion
½ cup diced red pepper salt and pepper to taste

Directions:
Boil pasta until tender.
Mix mustard and vinaigrette.
Add rest of ingredients.
Serve chilled.

Remember, it isn't etiquette to cut any one you've been introduced to.

DEVILED GREEN EGGS AND HAM

Ingredients:

1 dozen eggs
¾ cup mayonnaise
2 thick slices of ham
salt and pepper to taste

2 tablespoons dijon mustard
1 avocado
1 teaspoon paprika
2 drops green food dye if desired

Directions:

Boil eggs in big pot (single layer) for approximately 10 min.
Once eggs are cooked, peel shell. Cut in half.
Remove yolks and put in medium bowl.
Chop up avocado. Mash avocado and egg yolks together.
Add mustard, mayonnaise, paprika, salt, pepper, and food dye.
Put yolk mixture back into egg whites.
Slice ham into strips. Roll up and put in eggs. Sprinkle with
paprika.

CUCUMBER SANDWICHES

Ingredients:
2 cucumbers   ½ cup chopped scallions
1 cup cream cheese   1 cup sour cream
Bread

Directions:
Peel and dice one cucumber. Thinly slice other cucumber.
Mix cream cheese and sour cream until well blended.
Mix in scallions and diced cucumber.
Spread mixture on slice of bread, add cucumber slices on top.
Sandwich together. Cut into four wedges.

RED ROSE SCONES

Ingredients:
Scones
3 cups all-purpose flour   ½ cup white sugar
¾ cup butter   1 egg, beaten
5 teaspoons baking powder   1 cup milk
½ teaspoon salt   1/3 cup of red jam
Glaze
½ cup powdered sugar   ¼ teaspoon rosewater
3 tablespoons whipping cream

DIRECTIONS:
Preheat oven to 400 degrees.
Mix scone ingredients in a large bowl.
Knead dough. Roll out dough and cut into wedges, or use
heart-shaped cookie cutter.
Cut scones horizontally and fill with jam. Place on baking sheet.
Bake for 15 minutes or until golden brown.
Mix glaze ingredients and drizzle over cooling scones.

TREATS FOR YOUR TEA PARTY

CRANBERRY RUM CUPCAKES

Ingredients:
Cupcakes

½ cup butter
2 eggs (room temp)
1½ cups cake flour
½ cup milk

¾ cup white vinegar
3 teaspoons rum extract
1¾ teaspoons baking powder
1 can whole cranberries

Frosting
1 lb sifted, powdered sugar   1 cup shortening
2 teaspoons rum extract   2 teaspoons milk

Directions:
Preheat oven to 350 degrees.
Put liners in cupcake pan.
Beat butter and sugar with electric mixer until fluffy.
Add eggs one at a time while mixing.
Mix in extract and cranberries.
Add baking powder and flour, mix well.
Stir in milk until smooth.
Fill cupcake liners ½ full.
Put in oven, cook for 20-25 minutes, or until a butter knife comes out clean.
Cool cupcakes completely.

Frosting:
Cream shortening until fluffy.
Mix in milk slowly.
Add powdered sugar. The more you put in, the thicker it is, thus also harder to frost.
Add more milk if the frosting becomes too stiff.
Add extract last.
Frost cupcakes once they are cool.

"You can never get a cup of tea large enough or a book long enough to suit me." --Lewis Carroll

PEANUT BUTTER BALLS

Ingredients:
½ cup peanut butter   1 cup powdered sugar
1 package of white candy coating

Directions:
Mix peanut butter and powdered sugar.
Form into 12 balls.
Freeze for 10-20 minutes.
Melt candy coating in a double boiler; or if using a microwave,
put in for 20 seconds, stir, repeat until melted. Be very careful
not to overcook.
Remove balls from freezer and place in coating.
Place on wax paper until hard.
Put in refrigerator to harden faster.

TARTS

Ingredients:
1 cup flour   ½ cup butter
1 egg, beaten   2 tablespoons superfine sugar
4 tablespoons water   red jam

Directions:
Preheat the oven to 400 degrees.
Mix flour and sugar in medium bowl.
Rub in the butter until the mixture resembles breadcrumbs.
Add the egg and water. Mix.
Roll out dough on floured board. Cut into round or heart
shapes and mold crust upwards. Best when used in muffin tin.
Bake for 10 minutes. Remove from oven.
Fill with jam. Return to oven 10-15 minutes, or until golden
brown.

DRINKS FOR YOUR TEA PARTY

LUSCIOUS FROZEN PUNCH

2 ½ cups white sugar   6 cups water

1 - 40 oz can pineapple juice   2 - 3 oz packages strawberry gelatin

⅔ cup lemon juice   1 qt orange juice

2 - 2 liter bottles lemon-lime soda

Directions:

In a large saucepan, bring water, sugar, and gelatin to boil.

Boil for 3 minutes.

Stir in all juices.

Divide into 2 or more separate containers and freeze.

Combine the contents of 1 container with 1 bottle of lemon-lime soda in punch bowl. Stir until slushy. Repeat with remaining portions as needed.

TEA

Mad Tea - black tea, sugar, honey, treacle, cream, toffee

Cheshire Cat - Sassafras tea, vanilla, cream

Red Queen - ⅔ raspberry tea, ⅓ ginger ale, splash of grenadine, garnish with maraschino cherry

Drink Me! Tea - ⅔ Chamomile tea, ⅓ cranberry juice (very tart), may reduce size and blood pressure

ALCOHOLIC TEA
Alcohol may be added to tea for dueling purposes.

Queen of Hearts - ⅔ white tea, ⅓ rose hips wine

Golden Afternoon - ⅔ Yunnan Red tea (its golden tips produce a brassy golden orange color), ⅓ dandelion wine

White Rabbit - ⅔ white tea, ⅓ Moscato still white wine

Caterpillar - ⅔ green tea, ⅓ tequila with worm

Mushroom Tea - ⅓ Pu-erh tea (earthy aroma mold tea), ⅓ Lapsang souchong tea (smoked tea), ⅓ apple brandy, reishi medicinal mushroom

Looking Glass Tea - ⅔ Earl Grey, ⅓ plum wine, add unicorn horn or lionsbane as suited, drink backwards

White Knight - ⅓ Russian Caravan tea, ⅓ vodka, ⅓ coffee liqueur, cream

ACKNOWLEDGEMENTS

Author: Khurt Khave
Costume Designer: Johnna Buttrick
Photographer: Song River
Photographer Assistant: Becky Bradley

Models:
Alice   Johnna Buttrick
Jackie   Ashlynd Fine
Caterpillar   Tim Holt
Cheshire Cat   Khurt Khave
Queen of Hearts   Tiffany Kieft
Mad Hatter   Bryan P Miller
White Rabbit   April Walterscheid

teadueling.com

Made in the USA
Las Vegas, NV
14 November 2023